GET LOST, BECKA!

WRITTEN BY
SHIRLEY SIMON

ILLUSTRATED BY
DORA LEDER

Jenny is my big sister.

Jenny says I am too little.

Jenny says I am too little
to ride my bike with her.

Jenny says I am too little to skate with her.

Jenny says I am too little
to play with her friends.

Jenny says, "Get lost, Becka!"

Some day I will not be too little.

Some day Jenny will want to play with me.

But I will not play with her.

I will say, "Get lost, Jenny!"

Jenny will be sad.

I will say, "Don't cry, Jenny."

Jenny and I will play together.

See how much fun we have together!

The End